WD

SECRET TREE FORT

Brianne Farley

WALKER BOOKS
AND SUBSIDIARIES
LONDON • BOSTON • SYDNEY • AUCKLAND

It's a beautiful day! Go play outside!

Hi.
Are you reading a book?
Are you almost done?

Are you ready to play
with me?

Pleeeeeeeeeeeeeeeeease?

FINE!

I can play by myself.
It will be great.
It will be even better than if we played together.
I know just where to go.

I HAVE A SECRET TREE FORT,
AND YOU'RE NOT INVITED!

Did you hear me?
A secret tree fort.
It's cool. I mean really cool.
I bet you want to go there.
I bet you wish you were invited.
It is way up in the branches of
a super-secret tree.
It's a tree near here…
but I won't give you any
more clues.

And it's not just any old tree fort.

There is a rope ladder I can pull into the fort and a
water-balloon launcher JUST IN CASE OF ATTACK.

I'm serious! I'm NOT making this up.

I wish I could tell you more about it, but I can't.

It's a secret.

I never have to leave
if I don't want to.
If it rains, that's OK.
I just go under the roof.

If I want to look at
the stars, there's a
trapdoor in the roof
on the second floor.
And if I want to sleep
there, I can because
I'm not scared.

There's even a basket for snacks and other emergencies.

Inside the fort, there's
a marshmallow and
chocolate storage
compartment,
lots of maps,
and a walkie-talkie.

There are also different flags that mean different things
so I can call for backup.

One flag means
HELLO!

One means
HELP.

One means
OUT FOR SNACKS,
COME BACK LATER.

If there aren't any attacks that day,
there's a magnifying glass for looking
at bugs and other cool things.
Very cool things I can't tell you about.

part of a monarch butterfly wing

an oak leaf the same size as my face

cool twine

a p

another leaf

a broken eggshell

a smaller leaf

a lightning bug

sea monster tooth

little shells (how did they get in the woods?)

rough bark

smooth bark for passing notes

KRISTIN

...tle (pom-poms for bugs)

beach glass

gold doubloons

a turkey feather

moss

a wishing rock

a tiny rock

a very soft feather

a cicada

a rock that sort of looks like a heart

an old sweet

I wish I could.
But it's a secret.

If I stand in the crow's nest, I can see the ocean, so I know how many whales pass by and whether there will be pirates.

YARR!

When there are no pirates and lots of
whales, I can go down a secret tunnel
to the underwater viewing area.
And I hang out with the whales and
we play board games together.

Can you imagine anything better?
Don't you wish you were invited?
Doesn't this sound like the best
tree fort in the world?
And I haven't even told you the best part!

That doesn't exist.

Yes, it does.

No, it doesn't.

Fine!
Maybe I made it up.

Well, maybe…

maybe we just need to build it!

For my
favourite sister

First published 2016 by Walker Books Ltd
87 Vauxhall Walk, London SE11 5HJ

2 4 6 8 10 9 7 5 3 1

© 2016 Brianne Farley

The right of Brianne Farley to be identified as author and illustrator
respectively of this work has been asserted by her in accordance with the
Copyright, Designs and Patents Act 1988

This book has been typeset in Filosofia

Printed in Malaysia

British Library Cataloguing in Publication Data:
a catalogue record for this book is available from the British Library

ISBN 978-1-4063-6723-2

www.walker.co.uk

MIX
Paper from
responsible sources
FSC® C012700